TIME STANDS STILL
FOR NO MAN

Corrina Lunn

DEDICATION

For Nick

CONTENTS

CHAPTER 1: THE WATCH

The first sensation Wes was aware of was rain gently splashing on his face. It was swiftly followed by the coppery taste of blood in his mouth and pain resembling a thousand volts of electricity surging through his body.

Sounds began to filter into his ears and he became aware he was lying on the ground. He opened his eyes and then closed them again rapidly as the pain of bright lights seared through his head. He wasn't sure what had happened, only that it was something awful.

He could hear noises around him. The metallic chatter of radios punctuated by voices filled with urgency and authority. Wes was tempted to stay where he was; to tune the noise out and sink back into the seductive velvet darkness. But the pain and rain conspired to keep him awake, and so, reluctantly, he opened his eyes. With difficulty, gasping with pain, Wes pushed himself upright and looked around.

As the scene around him came into focus Wes cried out, trying to make sense of what he saw. He tried to stand to improve his view, but his legs would not support him, and he fell to his knees again in despair. He could see the flashing lights of emergency vehicles. They concealed his surroundings in shadow before cruelly throwing them into stark relief. The neon-blue strobing picking out every soul-breaking detail. The scene clicked on, off, on, off but he saw enough; more than enough.

Wes saw an unfamiliar dark grey car. The engine was silent and the bonnet crushed. The driver, an older man with grey hair, was stood next to it. Blood was running from a large gash on his face, but the man was oblivious to it. He was talking animatedly to a policeman; hands gesticulating wildly and voice raised as he tried to explain what had happened. Wes heard the words, 'came out of nowhere'.

Wes looked away… his eyes came to rest on something further down the road. He shuddered as he recognised the car; the white Ford Galaxy he had been driving for the last year. It was on its roof, windows empty of glass, its' metal body crumpled and broken. Wes had a brief flashback to when he'd bought the MPV, chosen for its reliability and economy. The driver's seat, set high in front of a panoramic windscreen, made him feel as if he was king of the road. Now, that same car was reduced to a heap of crushed metal and shattered glass, fit only for the scrap yard. Firemen aimed jets of foam over the Ford's engine to stem the risk of it bursting into flames. Wes didn't know how he came to be so far from the wreckage. He assumed he had been thrown from the car in the crash, but he could not remember.

He could not remember!

Looking at the mangled remains of the car he could see that it was impossible for anyone else to have survived. Hot tears fell from his eyes and mingled with the rain on his face as he pictured each of the car's occupants…

His wife Amelia, beautiful both inside and out. Her smile brightened any room and lifted his heart even on the darkest days. She had a gentle way with children, especially their own. Her dark shoulder-length hair swung as she walked; especially when she leaned forward to kiss him. Her body curved in ways she professed to hate and yet he loved. She had light blue eyes that sometimes sparkled with merriment and sometimes darkened with sorrow.

Catherine, his beloved eight-year-old daughter with delicate and elf-like with long blonde hair that reached to her waist. She moved gracefully, always dancing as if music played in her honour wherever she went. She was a combination of her mother's grace and kindness and her own childish bravery. Wes had always believed that Catherine would take on the world and win. She looked at him, her daddy, as if he was the hero of the world and he wanted it to be true.

His son, David, Catherine's twin, younger by only 17 minutes and yet still the baby of the family. Wes saw David as a mirror image of himself; a dreamer with big ideas. David had fought to come into the world, barely breathing when he was born. Wes remembered the harrowing moment the nurses had rushed to resuscitate his son. He was so tiny and so fragile. David had proved them all wrong and had grown into a strong, intelligent boy. His curiosity knew no limits, and he was forever trying to work out how and why things worked, and what could be changed. David too was a child who could change the world if he only had the chance.

These three people were the precious cargo Wes had been responsible for, and he felt a sad desperation pierce his soul. He could not, would not, be guilty of stealing these precious gifts not only from himself but from the world.

As he watched the firemen crowded around the wreckage he knew this was his fault. He had been driving, even when he knew he shouldn't be. Everything came back to him in an instant. The feel of the steering wheel beneath his hands. The worried looks on Amelia's face and her biting her lip to avoid an argument. The way he had pushed the car further and faster in response to Amelia's unspoken recriminations. The arrogant way he had thrown the vehicle around bends, believing he was completely in control. The deception he had practised to conceal his weakness, lying to his wife, lying to himself. It was this which had brought him to this place.

Wes fell forward. Bile was rising in his throat, competing with the sobs that rose from his chest. The sobbing rendered him incapable of moving in a way that alcohol never had. What had he done?

Wes watched and listened as the scene unfolded before him. He heard the sympathetic voices of the firemen. His heart broke as he watched a big, broad fireman lift Catherine's body from the wreckage of the car and lay it tenderly at the side of the road. The fireman rose to his feet, wiping away tears, dislodging his helmet with his large hands. The fireman paused for a moment to compose himself before turning back to continue his work.

Wes could not look away. He was compelled to bear witness

to the scene. The fireman, bulky in his uniform and surely a veteran of many tragedies, lifted another small, broken body from the wreckage. Beneath the blood and dust, there was a gleam of blonde hair. The fireman laid David's beautiful, lifeless body next to that of his twin. Side by side as they had been in the womb, and for many nights since. Wes and Amelia had often checked on the twins to find them snuggled together in one bed, peaceful in a deep sleep. United in death, the children were serene in a way they had never been in life. When they were alive, happiness, merriment and joy had always lit their faces. Death had turned them into pale alabaster replicas of themselves; their faces still and unmoving.

Wes crawled through the mud and reached forwards to touch the lifeless faces of his children as if to check that they were real. A sob tore from the depths of his soul as he touched the still warm faces that would never move again.

Wes sat next to his dead children and watched in disbelief as the firemen lifted an unrecognisable mess from the wreckage.

Amelia's beautiful face, the face he had known for nearly twenty years, was mangled and twisted beyond recognition. Blood dripped from a thousand cuts. Her face was distorted from the impact against the windscreen. The same big fireman, his face still wet with tears, placed Amelia reverently next to the twins. He drew a sheet over the three of them, tucking them in as if they were only sleeping; as if they might wake if disturbed by the gentlest breeze.

The fireman paid no attention to Wes as if he knew the man needed to be alone with the enormity of his grief. Or perhaps the fireman could smell the alcohol on his breath and knew he was responsible for this bloodshed.

Wes looked at the three bodies huddled under the sheet and remembered cosy movie nights, the four of them snuggled together and giggling. He remembered the nights when Amelia had snuggled with the children because he had been drinking and she did not want to be with him.

Pain tore him in two as he remembered the joy of being a family. Playing board games together. Rushing through the school run. Listening to the twins' chatter to each other. Bedtime stories and helping with homework. He remembered the times he had hidden from them, so he could drink because that was what he needed. He thought, if he thought at all, that there would always be other times for games, movies or just being together.

Amelia, David and Catherine were now together forever; there was no more time for movies or games. This was not a Disney movie with the usual happy ending. Through his own actions and the hand of fate, he was alone and that could not be changed.

Wes fell forward, his soul and heart in agony. He placed his hands on the cold wet mud to steady himself. Almost subconsciously, his fingers dug and scratched the earth as if to burrow into it to cover his shame, or perhaps to dig his own grave. His fingers dug deeper into the cold, wet mud as he sobbed. How could he live with the knowledge that his actions had led to this; the destruction of everything he loved? He closed his eyes, but he could not escape the images he had seen. The cold, still faces of his children and the broken body of his wife burnt into his memory. The woman he had loved for twenty years. The woman who had given him two amazing children to make his life complete was gone, and the pain was unbearable.

Wes howled into the night; a cry full of pain, shame and fear. He felt as if his soul had died, for without them he could not go on. His cry echoed through the night, seemingly unheard.

Wes was on his knees, his hands desperately scrabbling as if to seek purchase in this new reality. A world without his precious family. He only became aware of his fingers when they brushed against something hard and colder than the earth which concealed it. Working of their own accord, his fingers explored and pushed the dirt until they uncovered the object. His mind detached from his actions until he held the object in his hands and looked down. His hands clasped a dusty, silver lump. As he turned it over and brushed the last few grains of dirt from it, he realised it was a watch. It seemed old, antique even and was far more elaborate than any modern watch he had ever seen. Not at all like the simple Sekonda on his wrist. The watch's face was embellished with Roman numerals. The thick silver case was decorated with elaborate swirls and mysterious symbols engraved into the silver with delicate precision. An old, dirty chain hung from the watch, suggesting it was a pocket timekeeper, and it felt heavy in his hand. In places, the casing was worn smooth, as if it had been handled and inspected many times over the years. The strangest thing was, that although the watch had been buried in the soil and its appearance suggested it was old, Wes could hear the cogs inside. He looked at the watch curiously; studying it for several seconds. He could not see the ornate black hands moving around the watch's face, yet it was ticking. A quiet but clear tick, tock, tick, tock…

As Wes held the watch tightly in his hands, he forgot for a moment the tragedy that had unfolded before him. He focused on the watch, listening to the quiet sound that emanated from it; tick, tock, tick, tock… The watch shimmered and grew hot in his hands; so hot he almost let it drop. Wes blinked. The watch hands seemed to move: the large hand was at 6 while the small hand was nearing the 10: It was 10.30?

Wes was surprised. He was sure that hadn't been the time on the face before. Yet if asked, he would struggle to say what time the watch had said. Why 10.30 though? He struggled to understand the significance of that time: his mind full of the images from the past few moments. Why had he found the watch, what did it mean? Was there any significance to that time?

He felt dizzy as he realised that 10.30 was the moment this nightmare had begun. This was the time he had made the decisions that led to the death of his family. His beloved children, his gorgeous wife; grief almost overcame him as he remembered what he had lost. Every fibre of his being strained towards the watch. He yearned to bend the very fabric of time and space so that it was earlier, and not too late to change decisions made and save his family. If only he could turn back time; he could set this right.

Wes felt a breeze stir his hair, and a wave of nausea hit him. He rocked sideways, the watch clasped tightly in his hands. For some unfathomable reason, he did not want to let go of the watch, even though it would leave his hands free to steady himself. Instead, he held tightly as if he was clinging to a rope in a stormy sea. Wes did not dare to open his eyes, for he had already seen enough of the painful scene around him. He would never forget the sight of his wife and children lying lifeless at the side of the road.

As he sat, clinging to the watch, the sounds of the road grew more distant. The swish of tyres on the tarmac and the crackle of emergency radios grew quiet around him as if the volume was being turned down. There was a brief moment of silence. Then other sounds filtered into his ears; sounds which were familiar. Wes had a sudden feeling of déjà vu. Familiar voices calling goodbye, music in the background, people laughing and glasses chinking, and then the sound he wanted to hear most of all; a familiar voice heard every day for the last 20 years, now tinged with anxiety.

CHAPTER 2: THE FIRST TIME

'Wes, are you alright?'

Wes kept his eyes closed. He was scared that if he didn't he would realise he wasn't dreaming; that the nightmare was real.

'Wes, are you OK?'

The voice was now tinged with exasperation, suggesting the person speaking was beginning to lose their temper. Wes had no choice but to reluctantly open his eyes.

Amelia stood before him, concern in her eyes and etched on her face, the red and white dress she wore now creased from the day's activities. A wine glass in her hand, she looked at him closely and then sighed with disappointment.

Wes, on the other hand, had never been so relieved to see her. He bit back a sob and reached forward to touch her, to ensure she was real. She stepped back out of his reach, clearly annoyed with him. His hand faltered as he reached for her. He looked around in an effort to disguise his disorientation. Wes saw his cousin standing at the bar, deep in conversation with Wes' nephew Ben and his new wife Beth. Ben threw back his head as he laughed, his arm around his new wife's waist. Beth smiled up at her husband, relaxed now that the formalities of their wedding were over. She was still wearing her wedding dress, the white silk, reflecting the room's lights, rustled as she moved. Ben had removed his tie and loosened his shirt and looked far more relaxed than he had hours before as he waited for his bride to make her way down the aisle. Ben caught his uncle's eye and smiled, raising a hand in greeting, before turning back to the conversation. With difficulty, Wes turned his attention back to his wife.

Amelia was beautiful, he realised. He wondered when he had last looked at her properly. Her blue eyes were the same light blue as his children's; the colour of cornflowers and sapphires. They were now enhanced by expertly applied make-up. Her hair had been pinned up high, but a day of chasing the children and dancing had loosened the pins and tendrils now hung around her face. Her lipstick was the same shade of red as the poppies on her dress.

Wes shivered as the image of her broken face, covered in blood, popped into his head. He let out a raspy breath and shook his head to clear the image. When he looked at her whole, beautiful face again he realised she was annoyed. Really annoyed.

'Wes, I asked you a question!' Amelia snapped, her full lips pinched together. She was trying to control her temper, he knew, for Amelia hated public scenes.

'Sorry,' Wes replied. 'I was miles away'.

'Well that much was obvious' Amelia replied, before repeating the question, 'are you OK?'

Wes answered her with a nod, then asked 'where's Cathy and David? Are they OK?'

Amelia sighed, then replied 'they're fine. They were dancing with Elliot and your father last time I saw them. I've been talking to you for the last five minutes!' she added, the exasperation again creeping into her voice. 'You weren't listening at all!'

Wes tried to find the words to placate her, to explain what had happened, but he just couldn't. He wasn't even sure what had happened? Had he dozed off and dreamt it? Had it been a premonition, a warning or was he finally going crazy?

He realised Amelia was still waiting for him to speak, but then she sank down into the chair opposite him and suddenly looked close to tears.

'I thought this might be too much for you' she commented, 'it's still so early in your recovery and this isn't a situation where you can avoid alcohol. No one could blame you if you failed, but you need to be honest with me.'

Wes thought back over all the arguments that had taken place over the last six months since Amelia had found out he was drinking heavily. She'd suspected for months, had asked him several times and accused him of drinking too much. He had always managed to convince her he was just tired, stressed or had a headache. Even if she didn't quite believe him, he had been so belligerent that she had dropped it, tired of arguing. On the occasions Amelia had persisted, saying she was worried or asking how much he had drunk, he had lost his temper and called her names. He'd tell her she was overly sensitive and imagining things, or if he was snappier than usual it was because she was being awkward, or argumentative, and he was responding to her mood.

He found a million ways to hide his drinking. He kept glasses in the fridge where they were less obvious and could be topped up at will. When that raised questions, he began leaving bottles and cans in the back garden, so he could drink when he went out for a cigarette, put the rubbish out or to check the back gate. There were hundreds of reasons to leave the house. He hid bottles in various places where he knew Amelia would rarely look: behind the freezer, or on top of the wardrobe. It was only after months of arguing that Amelia had emptied the bins in desperation. She had done it when he was out, and he returned to find the bins on their side, rubbish strewn across the garden and the hard evidence piled up. Amelia had counted all the bottles and cans and confronted him. He had no choice but to admit that he was drinking more than he should, more than he admitted to. Amelia had then thrown him out.

At first, Amelia was so angry she refused to speak to him, except to arrange access to the children. Wes was devastated. His visits with Cathy and David were overshadowed by the thought he had to leave them. He imagined the times he wasn't with them, the bedtimes he missed. Wes held it together while he was with the children but when he returned to his empty flat, he sobbed. He sometimes drank as well, the vodka numbing the pain, but it didn't hold as much attraction as it had before. He also thought about Amelia; the pain he had caused her, the loneliness she felt. He wondered if she was alone and if she would ever forgive him. Gradually, Amelia had thawed and when he agreed to go to alcohol counselling she let him move back in. Wes and Amelia found their way back to each other, slowly and uncertainly, back to normality together.

They had talked a lot about this wedding. Wes was sure he wanted to go. Ben was his only nephew and he wanted to be there to see him marry the woman of his dreams. Wes had met Beth on several occasions and knew she was a good match for Ben. She was warm and hard-working and obviously loved Ben. Amelia was worried that an event such as this, with champagne toasts and an open bar, would be too much temptation for Wes. He assured her he could manage, that nothing was more important than being with his family on such a special day.

Amelia now leaned forward and gave him a small, sad smile. 'I promise not to be angry, I know how hard you've been trying. You promised, though, that you wouldn't lie to me again and I need to know the truth. Have you been drinking? If you have it's OK, I just need to know'.

In a fit of bravado, Wes had promised to stay sober so that he could drive them all home at the end of the evening. Amelia had been very doubtful, but the alternative was staying over at the hotel or taking a taxi, which would cost a small fortune they could hardly afford as the wedding venue was about 30 miles from their home.

Wes thought back to the wedding. It seemed he had lived a lifetime since then. He had seen his loved ones die and had then seen them resurrected. He struggled to remember what was real, but he remembered going to the bar several times, always when Amelia was busy with the children. Each time he had ordered a double vodka and a diet coke. The vodka to down quickly at the bar and the diet coke to take back to the table he shared with Amelia. The smooth vodka had slipped down his throat; warm and calming. It gave him the confidence he needed to face talking to people he hadn't seen for years and had nothing in common with. He recalled that every time a waiter had passed with a tray of champagne, he had taken a glass and drunk it greedily; quickly in case anyone had seen him. The champagne bubbles fizzed in his throat and distracted him from his anxiety.

He wasn't an obvious drunk. Only those who knew him well, like Amelia, would think he had been drinking. He was able to look fairly sober, steady on his feet and articulate, if somewhat disconnected until he crashed and had to sleep. That was what worried Amelia now. Wes knew she was worried he had been drinking because he seemed sleepy and disconnected. To him, he felt so disorientated because of the watch and what he had seen, but she would never believe him. He knew that even before events had unfolded he was drunk and this conversation seemed familiar. Had Amelia accused him of drinking earlier, before the crash? Was this time the first time around? He couldn't remember, but it seemed likely: the watch had only delivered him to a time earlier in the evening, it hadn't changed events.

Amelia leaned forward again, obviously concerned. Wes looked at his hands and realised that the watch, cold and silver, and still ticking, was clutched tightly in his right hand. Wes buried the watch in his pocket and tried to think through the fog of alcohol and trauma. This was the moment, he realised. This was the moment he could change everything. He could be honest with his wife, despite the recriminations and disappointment that would follow. He knew how hurt Amelia would be if he admitted he had failed, if he admitted he had given in to his need for alcohol and broken his promise to never drink again. Being truthful would mean disappointing his wife, the person he loved and had loved for most of his adult life. He could predict with certainty the tears that would follow and the recriminations. Wes wasn't sure that their marriage would survive. If he was honest though, Amelia would keep the children safe. He knew she would never let them get in a car if he admitted he had been drinking. Wes thought Amelia would take the children and leave him, but that was OK. They might not be with him, but they would still be alive, and that was better than the alternative. His mind filled again with the sight of their cold, pale faces lying next to the road, the tears of the fireman, and he resolved to change this moment and tell the truth. He would lose them, but they would still be in the world. If he lied, he knew he would lose them forever.

Wes planned the words he would say; the words that he would use to explain that once again he had let his family down. He had given in to his need for a drink and had gone to great lengths to try and conceal his behaviour from Amelia. He would tell Amelia how many vodkas he had drunk and how many glasses of champagne he had downed. Amelia would be angry. He was prepared to face the consequences, to tell the truth, if it meant that Amelia, Catherine and David would still be in the world. He knew that when Amelia heard the truth she would look at him with hurt in her eyes and he would feel ashamed, deeply ashamed, for letting her down. At least that was better than the unbearable grief that had ripped through him only a short time before.

He could avoid the moment Amelia had loaded their innocent, trusting children into the back of the car that had taken them on so many adventures and would now become their death trap.

He could avoid the moment when spurred on by the reproachful look on his wife's face and Dutch courage, he had pushed down on the accelerator, driving the car ever more recklessly in a bid to prove he was capable.

He could avoid the moment when, lulled by the dark road before him and the alcohol in his system, he had fallen asleep at the wheel and the car had drifted across the midline of the dual carriageway.

He could avoid the moment when a blaring car horn startled him awake. That moment the oncoming headlights lit up the car's interior like a super trouper, focussing on David and Cathy in the back seat. They looked so peaceful and beautiful. They had so much potential and their light about to be snuffed out.

He could avoid the moment when his vodka-fuddled brain refused to react, and he did nothing to save his family. When the vision of the oncoming car overwhelmed his senses and he just sat there watching the nightmare unfold.

He could avoid the moment when he knew, without doubt, that they were going to crash.

He could avoid the moment when the oncoming car struck the Ford head-on, sending it into a terrifying helter-skelter over which Wes had no control. Wheels and metal screamed against the tarmac, sending bright sparks into the dark night around them. Wes saw the other driver's face, pale and scared, his mouth stretched wide in a scream that Wes could not hear above the cacophony of noise. The Ford continued on its helter-skelter ride, spinning onto its roof, smashing against the road, propelled backwards by the force of the other car. Wes could hear his children's screams as they awoke from their sleep. His children, full of innocent dreams, hurled into this whirling loud nightmare, full of noise and blood.

If Wes told the truth, right now, he could avoid the moment his wife's blood flew through the air as her head hit the windscreen. He wouldn't hear her bones shatter above the noise of the crash and her beautiful face break. At least, he thought, she was unconscious and was spared the last few moments of this terrifying ordeal.

He could avoid the moment when he hung upside down, suspended from his seatbelt while the car sat on its roof. He heard petrol and blood dripping; drip, drip, drip; He opened his eyes and saw more headlights bearing down and knew there was nothing he could do.

He could avoid the moment when a second car ploughed into the side of the Galaxy, pushing it further along the road. His ears rang with the cacophony of metal against metal, of tyres straining against the road, and the screams of his children. Followed only by silence; except for the drip, drip, drip.

He could avoid seeing his beloved daughter lifted gently from the wreckage, the child he had cradled in his arms and sworn to protect for always. She looked as if she was sleeping peacefully, except for the river of blood that flowed down the front of the sparkly party dress she had worn that day.

He could avoid the moment his beloved son, the dreamer, the rescuer of insects, the star-gazer, was pulled from the wreckage and laid next to his twin, to sleep for eternity.

He could avoid feeling his heart break as they pulled Amelia's body from the wreckage. The body he had desired and shared for so many years. The body which had brought forth the children he loved with his every breath. No white was visible on her poppy-patterned dress. It was red; slick and dark.

He could avoid the moment when he realised his soul mate and his family were gone forever.

He could avoid the moment when an unknown, burly fireman cried over his wife and children while Wes sat, screaming; unheard and unseen.

CHAPTER 3: THE SECOND TIME

Wes took a deep breath. He would tell the truth, no matter what the consequences, for at least his family would still be alive. He looked at Amelia's face, etched with concern. Wes studied every beloved line and prepared to tell the truth. Even though it would cause her pain, and cause him shame, Wes knew that by changing this moment, by being honest and facing the consequences of his actions, he could avoid the horror of the moments that followed. Wes could not believe his luck, but somehow the fates had heard him, and he had found the watch. This dirty, old watch had taken him back and given him a chance to avoid those moments. It had given him chance to change the course of the night and save his children and his wife from their awful fate. Wes did not know where this elaborately engraved old timepiece had come from, but he thanked the Gods that he had found it. He took a deep breath and opened his mouth to say the words he planned.

Wes opened his mouth and started to speak, but he was shocked to hear that the words he spoke were not those he had prepared. Instead of telling the truth he heard himself spewing the same lies he had used so many times before.

'I'm fine' Wes heard himself say. 'I'm just tired, and we have a long drive ahead. We need to get going soon'. Wes cursed himself and desperately tried to stop talking. He wanted to rewind the conversation and start over, tell the truth and change the future. In his mind he had the words lined up ready to say, and yet, no matter how hard he tried, he just couldn't say them. It was as if he was watching a film, the screenplay already written, and he was just an actor allowed only to say the lines before him; no ad-libbing.

Wes took a deep breath and tried to start again. He used every ounce of his strength; every sinew in his body strained against the bonds fate and his own deception had placed on him. He heard his voice say 'Amelia' and his heart lifted: he could do it, he could save them! His heart then plunged into icy depths as he heard himself again convincing Amelia that it was time to go, that he was fine, he hadn't been drinking. If he seemed distant, unsteady, it had been a long day, his head was bothering him and he had found the day a real strain. He hadn't been drinking, of course, and he would get them home safely, but it was time to go. Wes railed against himself but to no avail. It was as if he was stuck behind a glass wall and although he banged repeatedly against the glass, the people on the other side could not see or hear him. His frustration and fear grew as he saw Amelia's face change, as she began to believe Wes' lies. Amelia's features softened, and she sounded concerned as she asked Wes if he was alright, did his head hurt badly and had he taken any painkillers? He hated himself for being so convincing, for knowing the words that would make her believe. Twenty years together had provided him with the knowledge he needed to assuage Amelia's fears. He knew the words to say and the tone to use; the actions that would help her accept that he was sober. He was fine, it was her imagination and the problem was nothing more than a headache. His mouth said, 'it's too warm in here, but once I get some fresh air I'll be fine'. His heart and mind told him that if his children got in the car with him they would die. This truth cut him into a thousand pieces, but no matter how hard he tried he could not make himself say the right words.

Wes cried inwardly as he watched Amelia round the children up, as they said their goodbyes to the many relatives at the wedding. It was a family occasion full of relatives; aunts and uncles, cousins. Cathy and David were flushed with the excitement of the day; their eyes sparkling and their cheeks pink. They laughed and giggled as they gave out hugs and kisses to the people still celebrating Ben and Beth's wedding. Wes screamed with terror and grief, his screams echoing in his head, bouncing off the inside of his skull. It was as if he was stuck in a terrible dream; a nightmare from which he could not wake up.

The hardest moment came when Wes' brother Nate and their parents, Cathy and David's grandparents, came to say goodbye. Wes' brother, Nate, was ten years older than him. Nate and his wife, Yvette, had been childhood sweethearts and had Ben when they were barely children themselves, but Nate had always been a devoted father and husband. They had been married for thirty years and Ben was their only child.

Nate and Yvette had tried for years to have another child, but it had never happened, and now they took great delight in spoiling their niece and nephew. Nate had beamed with pride during the ceremony and had unashamedly shed a few tears as his only son married the woman of his dreams. Wes watched, feeling sick, as Nate swung Cathy into the air and then delighted both Cathy and David by giving them a shiny pound coin each, tickling them and ruffling their hair. He could not believe that this was the last time his brother would see these children. He could not believe that his actions would lead to such devastation on what should be one of the best days of his brother's life. There had to be a way to change this? Surely, the watch had not brought him back for things to end in the same way?

Wes felt sick as his brother came to shake his hand. If he had been in control of his body he would have been on his knees, retching and pleading for forgiveness. Instead, he watched as his brother took him by the hand and led him slightly away from the group.

'I am so proud of you, bro' Nate said, his eyes gleaming and his face flushed from the many glasses of champagne he had drunk. Well, if you couldn't celebrate when your son got married when could you? Nate continued, 'I really thought you had lost it. I couldn't believe you were throwing everything away, you know? Amelia's a great woman and those twins…' Nate seemed lost for words and then continued, 'they deserve the best, you know? Take care of them, and next time, instead of bottling everything up and trying to drink your problems away, talk to me! I'm your brother, I've always got your back, you should know that!'

Wes' frustration turned to anger. His brother had known him

all his life; how could he not see what was in front of him? He was drunk, he wasn't safe to drive. Someone stop him! But Nate didn't seem to notice as he was drunk himself. Wes knew that he was far too good at covering the signs of inebriation for Nate to see it: after all, he had been doing it for years. Wes could only watch in despair as he agreed with his brother and shook his hand, making empty promises and saying he would call him in the next few days. Nate hugged him, holding him tighter than usual, and then said goodbye. Wes did not want him to let go, but his brother hugged him and sent him on his way. Wes tried to hold on, to say something that would alert his brother, but time was unstoppable. He could do nothing except walk away from his brother towards his fate.

As Wes moved away from Nate he saw his parents cuddling the twins. They had celebrated their eldest grandchild's wedding that day. Wes could not bring himself to think of what the next few days would bring them. He imagined their faces as they found out that their youngest son was dead, and that he had taken their daughter-in-law and beloved grandchildren with him. Wes had always been close to his parents; his father had been in the army and his mother a nurse. Things hadn't always been easy when he was growing up. His parents had sometimes been on the breadline but, no matter how much they struggled, they had always provided for and protected their children. They had tried to instil good values in both Wes and Nate. Wes knew they would be ashamed of his actions. He had not been able to bring himself to talk to his parents about his drinking. They knew about it because Amelia had appealed to them for help when his drinking was at its most obvious. His parents had never tackled him about it but they had been more present in their lives, trying to mitigate the effects of his actions. When he'd stopped drinking they had withdrawn not knowing he had only stopped temporarily. The call of the demon drink had been too strong for him to ignore forever. Wes knew they cared deeply for him and he did not want them to worry. Instead, he buried his problems and made sure they got no wind of it. His parents adored the twins and Wes knew if they thought they were in danger, they would do everything they could to keep them safe. He could not bear to think of the devastation this would bring on them. He knew their lives would never be the same, that they would never stop grieving for his children. He watched as his mother smoothed David's hair back from his face and planted a kiss on his flushed cheek. His father lifted his beautiful granddaughter high in the air and told her how beautiful she was. Wes felt ashamed of himself. Ashamed of his weakness. Ashamed of his need for alcohol that would destroy so many lives; his own, his wife and children's and every member of his family.

Wes saw a flash of the future. Ben and Beth wouldn't be able to celebrate their wedding anniversary without remembering the tragedy that befell their family that day. Nate and his parents would always blame themselves for what was to come, and yet it was nobody's fault except his. The trips to the cemetery his parents would make in the future. They would be grieving when they should be celebrating birthdays and graduations. They would never get to see the twins grow up to be the amazing adults that Cathy and David could be. Wes saw it all and wished the ground would open and swallow him in eternal hellfire for what he was about to do. He would rather suffer eternal damnation than inflict this pain on those he loved. Yet he still saw himself saying goodbye to everyone; faking sobriety; trying to walk in a straight line and not slur his words. Everyone seemed convinced. There was only one moment, a chink of light when his father suggested that they should stay over at the hotel. Wes cried with joy; surely his Father would stop them if he thought something was wrong? Yet again, he heard himself convincing everyone he was fine, becoming belligerent when people seemed doubtful until everyone gave up and accepted his explanations rather than have an argument. He wanted to scream or hit someone. He desperately hoped someone would stop them, would point out that he was too drunk to drive. No one seemed to notice.

Wes watched Amelia strap the children into their car seats, making sure they were securely fastened in. His heart broke as Amelia made sure that Cathy had her favourite toy in her hands and that David had his juice nearby. Wes tried frantically to speak, to stop this madness but no sound emerged. Instead, he watched his wife, his beautiful wife, strap herself into the passenger seat and look at him with trusting eyes, asking him if he was sure he was OK. He cursed himself for arguing so vehemently and cursed Amelia for believing him. She was a fool to believe him, but she trusted him. She loved him, and she would not, could not believe he would put them all at risk by driving if he was drunk. The man she had fallen in love with would never do that, would never knowingly risk his family. Wes watched, bile in his throat and his heart pumping with fear, as they pulled out of the parking spot. The children were still waving to those who loved them; the people who would be destroyed by what was to come.

The hotel car park was dark and quiet, and he tried to focus as he drove towards the gates. He pushed against the glass wall separating him from real life, and he thought he felt it bend. But he didn't have time to celebrate, he had to keep pushing until he was sure. Wes frantically tried to take control of his body. He felt his hands once more under his control, he could hear his ragged breathing, and he turned the car so that it would crash into the gate posts. He closed his eyes and braced himself for the impact. He felt the wheel move under his hands, and he heard the bonnet crunch as it hit the concrete gate posts. His heart rejoiced. At least this was only a fender bender, only the car was damaged and now everyone would know. But when he opened his eyes, they were turning onto the main road and the car was undamaged. It was as if nothing had happened, and indeed nothing had happened for Wes had no influence over his own actions. He could cry, he could scream and he could twist the wheel. At one point he tried to punch himself unconscious. He felt his nose crunch under his own fist, the blood dripping before he lost consciousness, but it was to no avail. Even though he experienced these things, that they felt real, when he blinked he was back in the driving seat and the car was cruising along. He saw Amelia's eyes widen with fear and heard the fear in her voice as she suggested they should slow down or pull over. His old self bristled with indignation and recklessness. Of course he was OK to drive, he had been driving for many years; how could Amelia have so little faith in him? Inwardly he cursed, shouted and punched the air around him, but his frustration and desperation had no effect. He could only watch with increasing horror as his wife became more scared, as he became more reckless.

The Ford glided through the dark streets like a ghost; streetlights flashing in and out of their view like a portent of the strobes that would light up the final scene. Even though it was late, there were several cars on the road and Wes cringed as he saw how fast he was driving. He overtook someone who was going too slow. He shook inside as he watched himself shake his fist and scream obscenities at the cautious driver. He saw Amelia's terror increase as she realised he was not himself. She realised that the demon drink was now in control of his body and his judgement. Amelia pleaded with him to slow down; to be more careful. He saw himself push the accelerator pedal down, taking offence at the insinuation that he wasn't safe to drive. In his head, Wes heard himself pleading, 'stop, for God's sake, stop! Tell her the truth, take a taxi, sleep at the side of the road but for God's sake STOP!' He could do nothing. He could only watch as he pushed the car further and further, throwing the Ford around bends as if it was a rally car; his drunken self, delighting in terrifying his wife with his antics.

Wes saw the headlights racing towards them a few seconds before the grey car hit them. He was exhausted from trying to change events, but he had stayed awake for this, the moment he dreaded. Wes closed his eyes and hoped it would be over quickly. He had tried to stop it. He had tried to tell the truth. He had tried to crash the car before reaching the road. Nothing had worked. There was nothing he could do except watch as everything that had happened came to pass again. The headlights, the car flipping, the screams, the sparks and metal breaking, and the blood cascading onto his face. The tears of the fireman as he lifted the twins' broken bodies from the car. The fireman's tenderness as he gently laid Amelia's body beside the twins and covered them with a sheet, as if they were only sleeping and would wake if the slightest breeze disturbed them. Wes sat next to his children's broken bodies for the second time and screamed at the darkness. He had tried, what else could he do?

Wes fell forward, his soul and conscience in agony. He placed his hands on the cold wet mud to steady himself. Subconsciously, his fingers worked ceaselessly, scratching the earth as if he was trying to burrow into it to cover his shame, or perhaps to dig his own grave. His fingers dug deeper into the cold, wet mud as he sobbed. He only became aware of his fingers when they brushed against something colder than the earth which concealed it. Wes knew what he was holding. He knew what he would find when he looked down. His hands clasped the dusty, silver lump which felt so familiar. As he turned it over and brushed the last few grains of dirt from it, he confirmed it was indeed the watch, gleaming menacingly in the dark. Wes hadn't noticed before, but now the watch's engravings looked sinister and threatening. Even though the watch had been buried for many years Wes could hear it; tick, tock, tick, tock, as if passing a judgement. The sentence he would have to serve. He had tried to change things. He had tried to take the chance the watch had offered him. Yet here he was, again, looking at the cold, still faces of his children and the broken body of his wife. Everything he had loved, his wife and children, were gone, and it was his fault; again. Wes howled into the night, a cry full of pain, shame and fear. He felt as if his soul had left, for without them he could not go on. His cry echoed through the night, heard only by the watch and measured by its relentless tick, tock, tick, tock…

CHAPTER 4: TIME ETERNAL

Wes closed his eyes and clasped the watch tightly. This time he would get it right. This time he would say the right words and tell the truth. This time he would save them.

He felt the wind. A wave of nausea rocked him as he heard the familiar noises; glasses clinking, voices calling goodbye, and an oh so familiar, oh so loved voice saying 'Wes, are you alright?'

He opened his eyes and saw his wife's beautiful, unbroken face looking down at him, exasperation evident as she repeated the question…

Wes had the opportunity to try everything he could think of. He tried drinking so much he could barely stand. He tried smashing a glass and using the jagged shards to slit his own throat; covering Amelia in a warm shower of his own blood. He tried walking away; leaving his family behind to walk through muddy fields to the motorway. There he stood in front of the oncoming cars, hoping for oblivion to come.

No matter what he did to try to change things, he'd close his eyes only to open them and find himself back in the car's comfortable driving seat. The panoramic view was again ready to show the way through the dark streets leading to his and his family's doom. The Ford Galaxy moved through the night like a living entity. It had a mind of its own; galloping towards its meeting with the grey vehicle as if it was a love-struck teenager.

Wes lived and died through that moment many times. He repeatedly saw the headlights coming towards them like a tsunami. His heart broke a thousand times as he watched the big, burly fireman lift his children's broken bodies from the car. Each time he a saw it was more poignant and final than the last. But it was never final. It was always there, to be relived over and over. No matter what he did or said, he could not change the actions that had led to the moment his wife and children had died. Because of his lies, and because he had been arrogant enough to risk their lives.

Finally, he realised that the watch was not there to give him the chance to change things. It was not offering him redemption. Its purpose was not to give him a second chance or to save his family from death. The watch's purpose was to ensure that he paid the price for his actions. To doom him forever to relive those moments that he would give anything to avoid. No matter what he did, he was stuck in the one moment he would change if he could. His sentence was to watch this moment on auto replay for eternity.

That realisation broke his mind, and he forgot to think, forgot to plan. He could only feel every ounce of the pain he had brought on himself and the shame and guilt he would bear forever.

He felt the wind.

A wave of nausea rocked him as he heard the familiar noises; glasses clinking, voices calling goodbye, and an oh so familiar, oh so loved voice saying 'Wes, are you alright?'

He did not open his eyes, for he knew what he would see…

BIO

Corrina lives in Blackpool where she is a Specialist Speech and Language Therapist, working with children under 5 years old with special needs, such as autism and eating and drinking difficulties.

She lives with her twins Ben and Emily and their ferret Bandit. The twins were diagnosed with Phenylketonuria (PKU), a rare inherited condition. Corrina and her late husband Nick did a lot of work together to raise awareness of this condition and, following the sad passing of Nick early in 2019, Corrina will continue this work.

Corrina is an avid reader and has been writing stories since she was young. She is an advocate of childhood literacy and believes children should be introduced to the world of books from an early age and be encouraged to write their own stories.

'Time Stands Still For No Man' is her first story to reach a public audience and is published for her family.

NOTE FROM THE PARROT

Corrina has been part of the Parrot family for quite some time - since she entered a short story competition for Phoenix Word Works - a Parrot cousin company. She has lots of books to write and we are discussing publication on an ongoing basis.

Sadly, early in 2019, Corrina's husband Nick passed away after a frighteningly short illness. His passing has left Corrina and her 10 year old twins Ben and Emily lost. The road they are now having to travel is being journalled in Corrina's blog which is published through the Parrot website. You can follow Corrina here:

https://www.purpleparrotpublishing.co.uk/corrina-lunn-blog

From a personal side, I did meet Nick on a few occasions. We 'gelled', as Corrina puts it. He was a very intelligent and kind man who loved music, especially Northern Soul. He was a well loved feature at many of the Northern Soul events held in and around Blackpool.

Nick Lunn, thank you for rekindling my love for this music.